**This book is for Emily.**

**Emily, we hope that the people who read this book are filled with the same joy and happiness that you share with us.**

**Love, Beck and Matt**

Little, Brown and Company

New York Boston

**The illustrations for this book were drawn and colored digitally. The text was set in Sentinel.**

 • Little, Brown and Company • Hachette Book Group • 1290 Avenue of the Americas, New York, NY 10104 • Visit us at lb-kids.com Little, Brown and Company is a division of Hachette Book Group, Inc. • The Little, Brown name and logo are trademarks of Hachette Book Group, Inc. • The publisher is not responsible for websites (or their content) that are not owned by the publisher. • First U.S. Edition: May 2017 • Originally published in Australia in 2016 by HarperCollins*Publishers* ISBNs: 978-0-316-43441-6 (paper over board), 978-0-316-43446-1 (ebook), 978-0-316-43582-6 (ebook), 978-0-316-43581-9 (ebook) • 10 9 8 7 6 5 4 3 2 1
APS • PRINTED IN CHINA

# Hello!

Do you have
favorite things?

I have favorite things.

They are bats and beaches
and bread and bushes
and bulldozers.

They are my favorites
because they all start
with the letter B.

**The letter B can make sounds too.**

**Can you say bububububub?**

**Can you say bobobobob?**

**Can you say brrrrrrrrr …**

**Yes, it is a bit cold in here, isn't it?**

**Oh dear, I think I'm going to …**

Aaaaaac

I think I'm catching a cold.
Excuse me.

Now, where were we?

Oh yes, my favorite things.

hhhoooooo!!!!

Here are a few more:

I love my _ed.

It's the _est _ed in the whole world.

My what?

Yeah, that's what I said.
Am I saying it wrong?

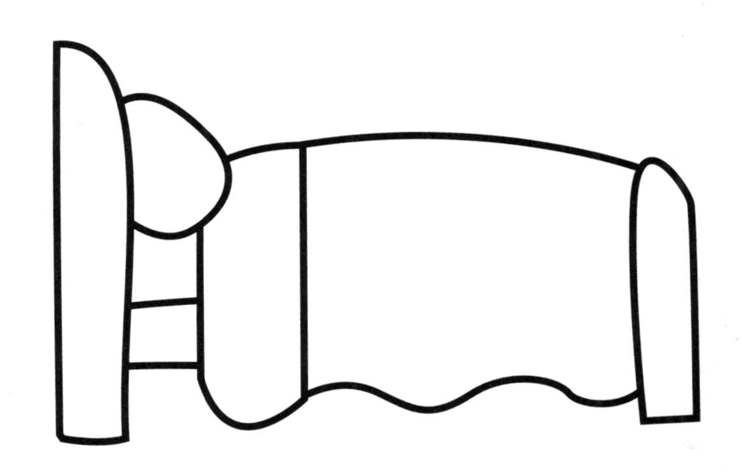

**And I like every size of _ull.**

**Hmmm . . . That didn't sound right.**
**Let me try again:**
**I love _ulls. Small _ulls and _ig _ulls.**

**I kick my _all whenever I can.**

**Oh dear. Something definitely isn't right.**

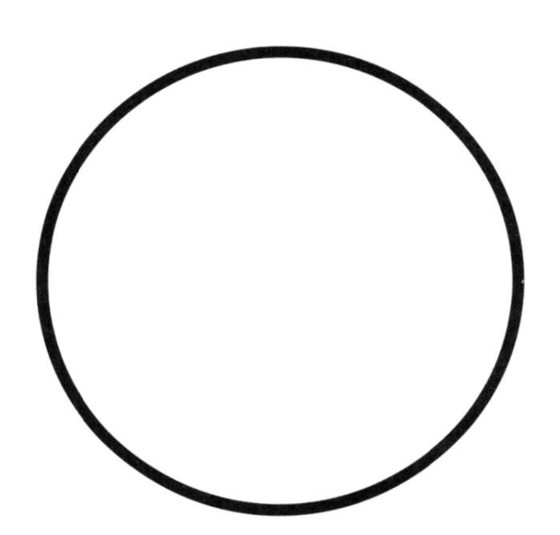

I think my favorite letter has gone from this _ook!

Let's check . . .

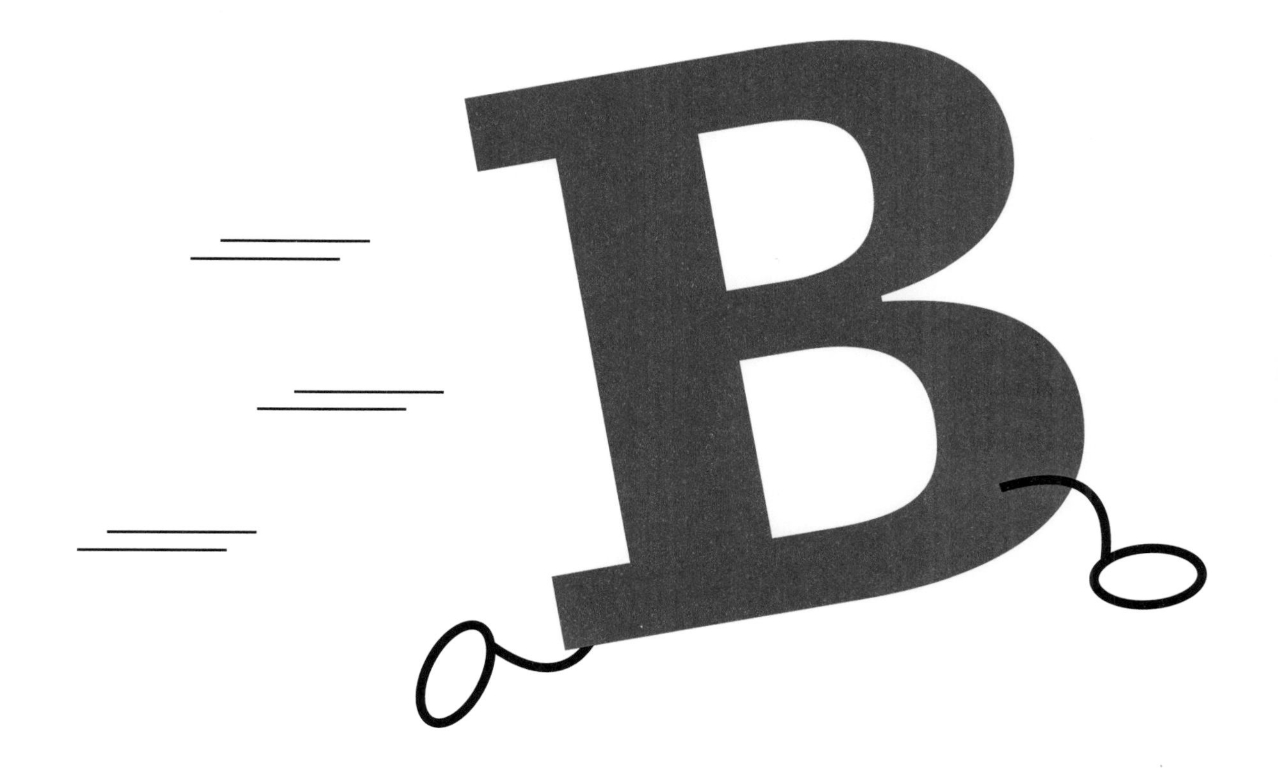

Look at this _utterfly.

Huh. _utterfly, _utterfly.
Can you tell me what that is?

Yes! A _utterfly.

**And look at this _eetle.**

**That's odd! It's still not there.
Is it there when you say it?**

**Oh, so it's just me, then?**

# Here’s a pair of _lue _oots.

**This is awkward!**
**Did you take my favorite letter from this _ook?**

**Where did it go?**

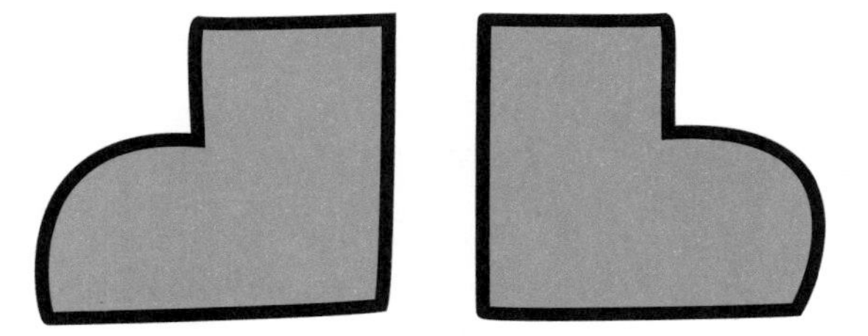

**Oh no!**
**Now the _eetle**
**is wearing the**
**_lue _oots!**

**What?**
**The _eetle is**
**wearing the _lue _oots**
**and jumping on**
**the _ed!**

# Uh-oh.
# Now the _eetle is wearing the _lue _oots, jumping on the _ed, and _ouncing the _all!

**I never realized how important my favorite letter was!**

**We really need it to come _ack to this _ook, don't we?**

**Look!**
**The _eetle is**
**wearing the _lue**
**_oots, jumping on the**
**_ed, and _ouncing**
**the _all with the _ulls!**

**Quick!**
**You have to help me.**
**Only you can say it!**

**Come _ack!**
**Come _ack!**

**Louder!**
**Again!**
**All together!**

# Come back

3!!!!

**Bravo!**
**Brilliant!**
**You did it!**
**You fixed it!**
**You put the B back**
**in this book!**

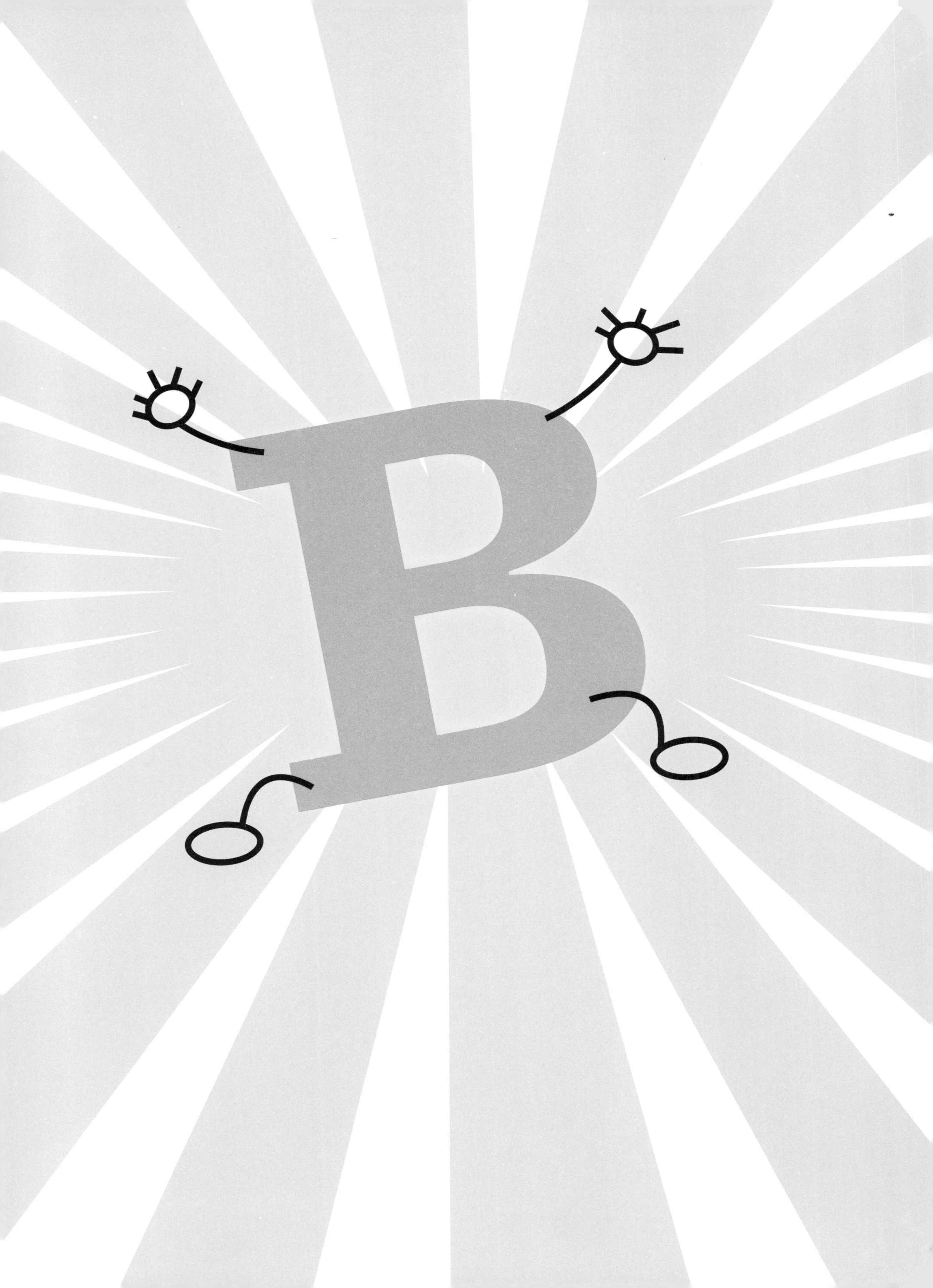
B